Broken Dreams

Broken Dreams

WL Gertz

Library of Congress Control Number: 2024921101

ISBN: 979-8-89228-272-7   (Paperback)
ISBN: 979-8-89228-273-4   (Hardcover)
ISBN: 979-8-89228-274-1   (eBook)

Book Ordering Information:
Atticus Publishing
548 Market St PMB 70756
San Francisco, CA 94104
(888) 208-9296
info@atticuspublishing.com
www.atticuspublishing.com

Printed in the United States of America

TABLE OF CONTENTS

LIKE GLUE

david and katie
one hundred beers and a bowl of hashish
a trailer, a shotgun, a red and white baby
a lighter, some worms and a fishing pole
everything begins at the end
how do you know
what you know?
is he suicidal or homicidal?
black beard and green sneakers
I'm afraid he's too quiet

Motorboats dribble / oil like spit on the lake
soup cans and lighting line the shore
the power is down / the stars are invisible
the fields smell of manure
and leftover rum

sun comes up like vomit over the hill
wind blows softly though the rotting trees
david and katie are sharing a cigarette
david and katie are looking at each other
david and katie are thinking of pain

how beautiful it is for those with servants
how beautiful it is for those with money
but oh what a life / for the salt of the earth

for david and katie
there is only a moment

THE AIR BREATHER

The wind carries dust voices
October rain enters
red, we do not believe what we see
white, aprons from Dayton to Dallas
blue, the story unfolds like a napkin
there are things we should never learn
never trust, never meet
we are out of control again
plunging like a frozen hart crane

Friday, heads feel warm, memories smile
the air breather looks for a crack in the wall
green, color of fate, our noble cause
brown, the bamboo king awakens
yellow, the sound of the earth crumbling

To die for the spring is a mortal sin
To die for winter is the final solution

TWO PHONE CALLS

Plants do not need water
They cannot read to save their lives
Garibaldi killed for freedom
We kill for chlorophyll

The Pope is murdered by the Arabs
As the Shroud is tested in Turino
Two million people in St. Peter's Square
Chant, "There is no X in comix"

The sky is light
The phone booth is melting
I slip outside
Liquid red dust remains
Where there once stood
An air breather

A DREAM IN A DREAM

Is all I can hope for
Red peppers seem tastier
Than they did in the sixties
Do unto others with
the time you have left

Curtail the words and
save them for eternity
Sparce and spare
Think of the alternative
As you fry in the wind

XEROX

One dimension, grey
it seems impossible
mind over matter
a two-sided reactor bends
to forces of heat and pressure
and brings back the past
the original years

god I remember my younger days
when life was unavoidable
put me under the wonderful rubber
silent, dark and green and black
dust free and airtight
spread my legs on the shining glass
the star like one-of-a-kind machinery view
is all I ever wanted
the time has come, the world needs others
copy me to pieces

BOATS

Between the lines
Between the times
I step, I crawl, I lie
There is beauty in what was to be
Alone, I wonder
Where is the beginning?
Where is the end
I smile, I weep, I fall
People are buying boats
In record numbers

CARE TOO DEEP

Before long
They chose between freedom
And cut diamonds
For forty years poetry
Meant death
Now it still means death
It doesn't change
It just changes the way
You look at the sun

Mad poets line up
For foreign cigarettes
California University sweatshirts
For life to be
The way it should
You need to look inside the castles
And become the walls

SNOW OF THE MOMENT

Hope doesn't spring
It leaps like a frightened fish
There are computers chasing me
Living my life to the fullest
Breaking aways means
Leaving it all behind
And I am ready to begin again
Without shame or self-pity

Can I refuse
The intentions on honorable thugs
Who die without warning
And live for themselves?
Or
Can I muse and melt with
The snow of the moment
While color and sound gently
Pull down my pants

LARRY AND ANITA

Larry and Anita
Met in Detroit
In Cobo Hall Arena on a Tuesday in June
Anita wanted a program
Larry proposed marriage
They wanted to see Spain but settled for Saigon

The Seventies were wonderful
For Larry and Anita
Cock fights in the dusk and pitchers of wine
Larry made sergeant
Anita made a baby
They tumbled to the floor
Playing Army at night

Larry made money selling cocaine to the troops
Anita helped with the packaging in her spare time
Silver foil ran out they switched to brown paper
Anita told the MP
Larry ran for the hills

Larry hid in the basement
Of a country estate
Owned by and Israeli with a wooden leg
Larry helped with the dishes and printed leaflets
Anita bought the baby a YSL blanket
Paid for by Friends of America

They met in a café in seventy-five
Two years without speaking
Two years without pain
Larry packed the gold for the Israeli
Anita fed her baby with no shame

They heard the guns and knew where to go
The Embassy was crazy the guards were insane
Situation hopeless
Sky turning black
Larry and Anita knew it was time

Their helicopter was not the last to go
Nor the first to take off from Saigon
Larry's borrowed gold paid for the flight
Anita's baby was part of the deal

Larry and Anita
A boy and a girl
The most modern couple in Detroit it was said
Look at each other and smile
But six months later
Neither would be dead

WHALING SEASON

There is a soft breath-like wind
Running through my hair
Beach sand is cold and clammy
The lifeguard strums his guitar
And waits for the word to leave

Whaling is almost in season
My harpoon is in the shop
Being sharpened for the fall

As a generation we are finished
Forever
No more us or them or them or us
It is finally, irrevocably over

The best of us could not
Buy the beauty of growing up poor
The worst of us decided to pretend
And took off their masks when the all-clear was sounded

Battles were never raged
Conflict was avoided
By the best of us
Who sit alone watching the world pass us by
Drinking Pina Coladas with the wrong people
For sport

OF PARIS

Should I buy two ships
And hang them out to dry
In an ancient world
Where I lived for a time
Or should I save
For eternity and my children
There is a noise in my head
clutter of the modern world
It does not stop - it's
One more tic and
One more tock
Surrounding me

AFRICA

The sun came through
Warmth on his knees
He thought of earlier days
As he sipped a foreign whisky

Dust in the morning
(which he always hated)
Before afternoons in the lush paradise
And early evenings studying
The poetry of his father

The largest moon he ever saw
Was paraded through his world
like a captured spy
The stars exploded and he felt a chill
And sweat on his brow like day-old raindrops

Alone with the animals
He could hear fur drying in the wind
But he was not afraid
The green grass would protect him
From the enemy whomever it was

And he would hear the humming of machinery
And that would be his lullaby
And only his rifle would remind him
That a Russian soldier
Was sleeping in Africa

(originally published in The Berkeley Poets Cooperative)

CAVES

What was it that drove her crazy?
Red sheets in the cave
Forty tons of unused materials
Fine sand all around

Sounds of birds
Sounds of pages turning
Father tells on me
His collar is dirty

Animals
licking
each
other

Misty snow death not funny, not funny
She jumps off the car
Into the garden
A photograph is snapped
Everyone is falling

THE ANNIVERSARY OF UNHAPPINESS

Information please 1983
Goodnight Florence
Have a good year
Highest recorded temperature
Woman's bowling championship
Kampuchea see Cambodia

Information please 1983
Francois Villon on a rocky beach
The ghost of Jack Ruby smiling at me
A GNP of 18 million
Per capita income of $230.00

Information please 1983
What year did what war end
How many colleges and how many students
Soaking up gravy and begging for more
There are Hessians alive in my boots

Information please 1983
Olympic standouts are out in the ditch
The coffee is burning
The water is rising
The bodies are lined up three deep at my door

Information please 1983
Goodnight Florence
Have a good year

POEMS OF ANOTHER ERA

Give me this day
One more memory
Of what could be

Alone in the chair
Watching water
Dry on plastic

That cars are obsolete
And money matters
More or less
Are poems of another era
Which come pouring out
For all to see

THE SUN AT MY KNEES

Running through pages of anarchy
Plotting courses on maps without America
I sing the sound of a thousand dead poets
and leap in through the gap in history
(Noble prize winners eating caviar
drop fish eggs into their greying beards)

Sitting in a café by the ancient baths
With visions of Romans building for God
I speak of the death of artistic drive
and leap in through the gap in history
(My wife is having a baby
its name is chocolate ice cream)

Standing in a room with no light to see
The paintings which are staring at me
I hum to dying cowboys and prostitutes
and leap in through the gap in history
(The bumps on the side of a basketball
are as deadly as those on a Neutron bomb)

Flying forty thousand feet in the air
with the clouds at my feet and the sun at my knees
I cry for the old and smile at the new
and prepare for my entrance into history
(Money flows like spit on a windowpane
while the young have dreams of eternity)

THE RACING NEVER STOPS

The racing never stops
Fooled by light and sound
And people all over
looking for me, looking for them

There is nothing important
There is nothing so important
as the opening of the flower
the sun bursting through the day

If I live to 100
I will not miss
My devices only
My brown hair
And friends I used to know

THE WINTER OF PAIN

In the Winter of Pain
when the sky fell faster
than an aging Superman
And the wind whipped
the men and women
waiting for the food truck

I searched for the sun
And what mattered most
And found what I was looking for
In the days of old

BATS IN THE PLUNGE POOL

Wired awake
Birds or bats
Cross view plunge pool
reminds me that
There is a God

Moving to the countryside
To carve santos
paint them for a collector
to come from the city

Me in thirty years

RENEGADE

For falling in love
the ancient way
The finer things in life
are gone

Like a bat in the breeze
a flower bends
opens its mouth
The paint chips automatic
like clay

RUSSIANS & POETS

When is the course of
human events
I wander off
Into the wilds
Holding a blue green camera
shooting away at
Separatists in the mist
Kicking up more dust

Fireflies of the moment
lighten my load as I
Yearn to be a better man
but fail in my quest

Large chandeliers
Of crystal & gold
Russians everywhere I look
Poets dying and being
reborn at last

ALWAYS A WINDOW

I rush to complete
Another episode, another
Way to see the future
Through the window
Always a window
For me to look through

I sing but never
open my mouth
Love what was and will be
Unafraid I sail
off searching for dry land
And the release of
Kings and Queens and
duty and honor
Movie and Television
Images all around me

Deep blues and reds
And songs and sounds
of everything and nothing
I am pleased with my fantasy
As life continues along its merry way

FOUND & NOTED

They play the same, the girls and boys
The dreams, the swimming
The ball crisp sound of kicking

Smiles and laughter
parents and grandparents chatter away
inhaling the moment

That it should remind me of my life
fifty years ago, is no surprise
As I wander off looking for adventure

Found and noted
Alone and together

I FORGOT THE SIM CARD

For one brief moment
I look around
And I see the past
All over
The days are few
For all it seems
I capture nothing
In print or form
There is no way
Out of this life I lead

RIBBONS

I am tired of pretending to be a ribbon
red and shiny/ curling at the ends
I want to be strong and live free and
believe in my immortality

Yet from my fire-escape, black tar burns and
bars divide the sky
I look up
The sun comes out and looks about
then begs to return to the clouds

I violently deny the existence of ribbons
and scrape the tar off of my face

I CARE NOT FOR KITES

While horses romp on the beach
And dogs have the ability
To frighten me

I care not for kites
While instruments gather dust
In basements to be uncovered

There are traces of people
Who meant little to me
Screaming my name
And asking me questions

Find me a way to
Leave without regret
This world, this irony, this moment

POSTART – REGARDS TO WILLIAM

hello from london
summer
i hope you get
cultured in europe (maybe even learn to spell)
you can't buy Marlboros in canada
sandy slonim was right
dave failed his driving test
can you believe it rained in arizona?
today we crossed the alps
nine hours of music and
ricard
will you be home soon
saw rabbit – he's fine
it's different here
slowly we turned/ no sign of duke mantee
684-1592
thank you
the sky very blue
back to the jungle/ off to trois rivieres
life is tough
regards to william

SUPPOSED TO BE

For a time, for a while
Life was all it was supposed to be
Sunny skies/ wildflowers/ walks
by the water's edge

Then the fall and winter pain
And round and round it goes
And if I die before I wake
My soul a shattered mess
Am I

Then a crack and a smile
An amusing tale of life underwater
Seagulls call an F sharp tune
Windowpanes/ mindful games
And a roller coaster feeling
Spreads like jelly on fire

There is a sliver, a slice, a peak
A way around, a way between
I hold my breath and dive in deep
Fish are electric/ blue and gray

CANDLELIGHT NIGHT

Needle marks understand the meaning of life
waiting in a crowded elevator shaft
for the Shah of Iran to give his order
"Spaghetti Vongole without the clams"

Blacks and Jews could give a shit
about the secrets of the sun
they murdered Harry Crosby and his brother Bing
Without a trial, without a care

3000 Russian troops in Cuba
sleeping with the daughters of family men
15 survivors in the Indian Ocean
Eating their children and watching TV

Mini-computers and Cartier watches
a shrink-wrapped life is all that we have
a package of this, a carton of that
a tax on our bodies, a lien on our minds

The world is what is used to be
but death comes quicker if you request it
love comes harder and we don't care
and history remembers the crack in the earth

TUESDAY

The air is soft like melting cheese
they sit by the docks and shoot dice all day
All mixed up and out of their grasp
and the red-haired boy and his dog

They try so hard to interrupt
the transfusion of liquid sound
The lines of beauty and the search
for the red-haired boy and his dog

Paint falls like a vacant dream
the sun turns to say "It cannot be"
And they try but can never quite reach
the red-haired boy and his dog

Under the covers to stop the pain
Their eyes fixed on pleasure and misery
They realize that the end is near
for the red-haired boy and his dog

Yet what day falls after Monday?
I scream as the red drips down on my eyes
What day falls after Monday?
I cry, embracing the boy and his dog

PARIS IN BLUE

Red wasp wings trapped in a misty glass
surrounded by the cheese of a Croque Monsieur
The paratrooper is trapped by the promise of a bed
and one thousand tri-color dreams

Life is expensive, but the tomatoes are ripe
French Foreign Legion lands in Zaire
Croissants are not what they used to be
For butter is scarce, and the massacre begins

Paratrooper remembers 1954
when they told him, "forget it, be gone"
Paratrooper remembers 1968
when they told him, "forget it, be gone"

He'll bleed red wine in the Café Le Ruth
for all the fucked-up people in this fucked up world
Block out the sun and cry for himself
For he'll never grow old/ He'll never surrender

Not while sugar comes wrapped in paper
Inscribed with the beauty of Paris in blue

THE NILE

She had a mouth like a rose
And waited at home for warmth
He spoke all day of bank notes
And in the evening, he gave her the stock exchange

It was so beautiful that I couldn't help
But cover the Andes
With last night's potato salad
The Nile with buttered noodles
Watching with sweet love
Under an August moon
I threw up all over the world!

MORE THAN FORTY YEARS AGO

Carelessly enter the Old Bakery Hotel
Cough bad, three days without a meal
'cept for peas, vodka and more peas
Did I lose it last week on the ferry to Holland
when the sea mixed with the vodka in my cup?

Or was it on the train to Bilbao
with the seven a.m. beer in my head?
Or was it at the lovely Old Bakery Hotel
where I finally came to rest
with those blue Swiss cough pills
Which made me sleep, sleep, sleep?

Oh God, is that you?
It is, I think, I need
more peas and more pills
and I must get out of this
evil fucking bakery of a (more hashish, thank you) city

Dutch sky blazing
eyes burning, burning, burning
Talk to yourself and not to the others
It's the secret of success and I know it

I walk quietly out of the Old Bakery Hotel
And throw my body into the oven

I am finally a loaf of bread

POINTS LESS WAITING

A smile returns
When it begins again
Beauty calls out/ waiting
No age limit in Kabul

For a second, I am back
Where I began
Bloomingdale nightmare/ waiting
Justice in the end

I am no longer satisfied
With poetic interruptions
When destiny becomes / waiting
A joke in the distance

WHOLE BLOOD IS NEEDED

Pacific Ocean rising like a river
rock 'n' roll flashes light in the sky
warmth flows smoothly and hugs the mind
the evidence is presented to the Queen of Siam
Still:

    The glorious circle only half-complete
    New manifestos partially filled
    Pinball computerized dreams
    And something is very wrong tonight

Down the street / chinese white
Someone is hurt/ firecrackers explode
hurt so bad, hurt so bad
Carry her out / watch the arm
the arm, oh the arm
Put the fingers in a Brillo box
and call for the King of the Bongomen

Traffic jam, go around, hurry
go 'round, but first
stop for a pizza and orange drink
too late for coffee, go find a nurse

Bright sun through the fog
daylight is here, but night has not ended

Whole blood is needed
all over the world!

BARKING DOGS

He almost
Killed himself because
I do not know
It's easy to ask but harder
To hear the answer

For years
We wondered
What color we should choose
Let barking dogs
Lie to you all night long

There is a quiet pain
Running free
Spanish situations
And sacks of potatoes
Hang me from a tree
And we'll kiss forever

MORE POINTS

Shooting the messenger
Reviewing a decade
Wishing snow turning
Into oat bran

Christmas is
A time to hide
Under exploding grenades
Made from the half-dead fish

Whether I should change this life
Is less important than
How many whips it takes to kill a bat

Quest for the nineties
Leave me alone

I QUIT MY JOB TODAY

Lost in London
Street names turning
To confuse me like wasted love
There is beauty in losing your way
Surprise in finding no hotel
Where it was yesterday

For five years the answer
Remained up my ass
Angry for realizing the
Way in, is the way out

Poetry, like empty money markets
Is a disease of the body
Not the mind
Think carefully before
You forgive the world

REMEMBERING WHEN

The unborn lie awake
as we dream of days
When we sat alone
A boxer hugs
an AIDS patient

Like a sailor on a sinking ship
ten years from this moment
the world will have forgotten
Teenage Mutant Ninja Turtles

I will remember when
My body was full of pain
And my mind an empty
Automobile

They cut the lilacs too deep this year
I will always remember when

SOARING

Is a message I'd like to find
higher than I've been before

On that ferry, on that train
going no place in particular

In the days before planning
I was
Soaring

You in my pack
was all I wanted
Still all I want
But the world gets in the way and
I never know what's real and
who is right

I know I want you
Soaring

THE REINCARNATION OF JUDY GARLAND (WOMEN IN THE GUTTER)

First, she smiles for me
then goes for the throat
I ask what is the difference?
and she spits in my eye

How can she raise children
on this cruel, dying planet?
How can love last
when she has to water it?

They eat voices for breakfast
and chew their way to success
As a fly lands on a table
and dies with dignity

All the deadly black and white
The chess game with the blind architect

But what of the grains of sand
the tiger's teeth
the wind carrying petals to the sea
the hospital corridors stinking of light bulbs
the quiet December morning in the blinding white
the blood of Algerians, the phlegm of West Indians
the whole human race running backwards?

It is the bratwurst of times
for the woman in the gutter
Who turn ancient heroes
into the corpses of the world

It is the complicated life of a woman today
ruling with a whip made of burning flesh
The complicated life of a woman today
waiting for the sun to burn out

TIME OF MY BEGINNING

Too real/ too bad
Ancient machines hum like goblins
Regain the touch/ fine china
Chip away like a blocked dream
On a snowy beach in June

There is a reason/ why
All things breathe
And children die
Purple days ahead/ gone by
Leading with sons and daughters

This is/ was the
Time of my beginning
Later than ever/ early
Morning sun shower
Hold a flower tight to my chest

Forward to runway number six

POINTS

Secrets, like chocolate,
Are good, then bad
I wonder why the noise
Never got to me before

A window, a spy, a patriot
All hold my attention
Like tulips in June

One quarter of my life
Was spent in limbo
Awaiting judgement
Never to come

Awaiting an answer
A song or a dream
Anything but tax tables
Running amuck

Secrets like chocolates
Are out of the bag
Waiting for instructions
Like seeds in the dawn

WHEN POETRY WAS KILLING TIME

Back in time, I go
To a place where
I once was for a lifetime
When I had
Three minutes of my own and
Poetry was killing time

The lines don't pour
They dribble out
So slowly
The exploding moments are gone
My eyes have it only
For those who never
Saw them before

The days of old
Are days of old
I see through nothing but
My own emptier eyes

INDEPENDENCE DAY

For one or three
I sing for the trousers
Of men long dead
Like fur traders of old
I study cases of long dead companies
Vying for the one
The one
The perfect sum

LEARN THE HARD WAY

She wonders if his powder is white enough
and laughs just like the peasants do
in a town called Blank at the Lizard's Bar
down the road from the Unhappy Hotel
a filmmaker spills a drink on a colored whore
a plumber beats his face in with a plunger
an MBA looks for an angle with a ruler
an accountant notes damage with a pencil
a poet has a beer and glides out the door

She looked at the moon and at Manuel
then she learned the hard way

IIn a broken-down Chevy in Medford, Mass.
he is surrounded by snow and bright white lips
is told by a Catholic with a green fedora
"find 93 or die, find 93 or die"
he turns on the heater and rolls up the window
carbon monoxide chill/ sweet, sweet smell
fifteen bucks more if he goes to Hell

He said they rolled Mexicans
not cigarettes on the Mystik Parkway
then he learned the hard way

In every city in every town
in Pittsburgh in Paris in Bangladesh
in Windsor in Waterville in the Panama Canal
in the back of the bank
in the front of the truck stop
in the middle of nowhere it's always the same
when the sun goes down, they let out the lions
and winners tell losers that their time is up
when the sun goes down, they let out the lions

It's not safe for a man with a hole in his heart

THE SOUND OF THE WORD UNSPOKEN

breaking another sacred vow
I explain it to myself once again
"what does it really mean?"
smile/ think of
hours on my back contemplating a branch
tears crawling down my face as I
stumble over a perfect line
hair pulling itself as I lose the ray
tender mind running always running
teeth-gritting vision unseen
hearing the sound of the word
unspoken
shaking, squirming, one more word
yes or no
never maybe
rain and the window – watch the snakes
and the blond
touch them/ touch her
they disappear and
it begins
little dots get longer and longer
inner, inner – stay in
come out

as if fame and fortune could ever tell
me so

as if fame and fortune could ever buy
me rainbows

MANIFESTO IN THE SECOND COLOR

speeding towards the 'eighties in a car without an engine'
the nineteenth century in the glove compartment
a pack of poems on the seat
soon the earth will be obsolete
no need to long for a mythical golden past
when you can bank 24 hours a day

no need to chase the future
when you can be a "productive member of society"
the present will have to do; stop fucking around!!!
don't be afraid to crusade
for art and the spark of genius that seethes in you

refrain: Johnny Carson is not the enemy, he is your
reflection in a poisoned lake...

They, slaves of the elements
conditioned by years of degree-days, call it spring
but don't be deceived; it means nothing
nothing at all
you don't have to buy an ice cream cone
because the sun is shining
you don't have to pretend that you're happy
because the weather is warm
only merchants love the heat
they have products to sell & minds to melt
don't let them tell you that you have nothing...
you have everything!
there is nothing else to buy, there are no finer things in life

summer is coming
garbage in the streets/ water for sale
suntan lotion/ neo-nazis washing their cars
oh, to be in paris, drinking ricard and watching bums eat fire
oh, to be in amsterdam
smoking black beauties and falling into the canals

we're getting out
or are we already there?

(co-authored by Steve Haggard)

The author was the co-founder of DREAMS, a poetry and music magazine in NYC in the 1970s and early 1980s. Many of his poems appeared there first. He backpacked through Europe in 1973 and 1974 which inspired much of his writing. He continues to travel extensively each year and enjoys cinema, modern art, and fencing.

www.ingramcontent.com/pod-product-compliance
Lightning Source LLC
Chambersburg PA
CBHW022115150726
47990CB00003B/1357